17.99

D0520339

Copyright © 2020 by Cale Atkinson

All rights reserved. Published in the United States by Doubleday, an imprint of Random House Children's Books, a division of Penguin Random House LLC, New York.

Doubleday and the colophon are registered trademarks of Penguin Random House LLC.

Visit us on the Web! rhcbooks.com

Educators and librarians, for a variety of teaching tools, visit us at RHTeachersLibrarians.com

Library of Congress Cataloging-in-Publication Data is available upon request.
ISBN 978-0-593-12280-8 (trade) — ISBN 978-0-593-12281-5 (lib. bdg.) —
ISBN 978-0-593-12282-2 (ebook)

Interior design by Nicole Gastonguay

MANUFACTURED IN CHINA
10 9 8 7 6 5 4 3 2 1
First Edition

Random House Children's Books supports the First Amendment and celebrates the right to read.

MONSTERS
By
Cale Atkinson
MONSTER
DOUBLEDAY
Doubleday Books
for Young Readers

You've heard the spooky stories, the rumors, the whispers.
It's time we shone a light on what *really* hides in the shadows.

Say hello to the masters of Monstronomy.

Bats and Blood Specialist

Goop Whiz

Moon Chaser

Expert on Brraaaiiinnnnns

These creatures of the night aren't here to frighten. They are here to enlighten! Will you be eaten along the way? Well, there's always a chance, so keep your wits about you and hold on to your juicy brain.

1: What Is a Monster?

So just what makes a monster a monster? Is it a diabolical laugh? A terrible smell? Or the fact that some of their teeth are longer than your legs? Let's find out!

OFFICIAL MONSTER CHECKLIST

EYES:

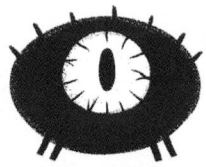

- [ ] One bloodshot
- [ ] Glowing
- [ ] Seven stink eyes
- [ ] Flaming pupils

BODY:

- [ ] Purple fur
- [ ] Fireproof scales
- [ ] Sticky slime
- [ ] Poison prickles

TEETH:

- [ ] Yellow fangs
- [ ] Gruesome tusks
- [ ] Pointy chompers
- [ ] Chunky chompers

FEATURES:

- [ ] Bony wings
- [ ] Gnarly claws
- [ ] Curly tentacles
- [ ] Jagged horns

CLOTHING:

- [ ] Spooky cape
- [ ] Old-timey duds
- [ ] Mud and leaves
- [ ] Ripped bandages

ODORS:

- [ ] Limburger cheese
- [ ] Raunchy toe jam
- [ ] Garbage juice
- [ ] Rancid leftovers

Is that a monster hiding under your bed?!
Use the checklist to be sure!

MONSTER FACT

Frankenstein is the name of the scientist who made the monster. The actual monster has no name!

Ahhh! I have no name!

What would *you* name him?

2: Biology

Now that you know *what* a monster is, it's time to dig deeper into what's going on beyond the fur and fangs.

Common name:	Monster
Scientific name:	*Super scarius*
Family:	Toothica Sharpidae
Territory:	Closets, crypts, dungeons, and under beds
Communication:	Grunts, howls, murmurs, and sneezes
Defense:	Teeth, claws, and slime
Name for young:	Furbs
Life span:	Forever, plus 4–5 years
Behavior:	Friendly, unless cranky

Unlike humans, monsters aren't limited to one brain, heart, and stomach.

As you can see from this durgle, the insides of a monster are just as interesting as the outside.
SORTING GULLET
SPOOKY SPLEEN
HAUNTED HEART
SWAMP STOMACH
MUNCHING BELLY
GRUMPY GIZZARD
EEL-TESTINES
SLIME BLADDER
LEFTOVERS
BARNEY

3: Monster Types

Monsters come in all shapes and sizes.

Common, everyday monsters include:

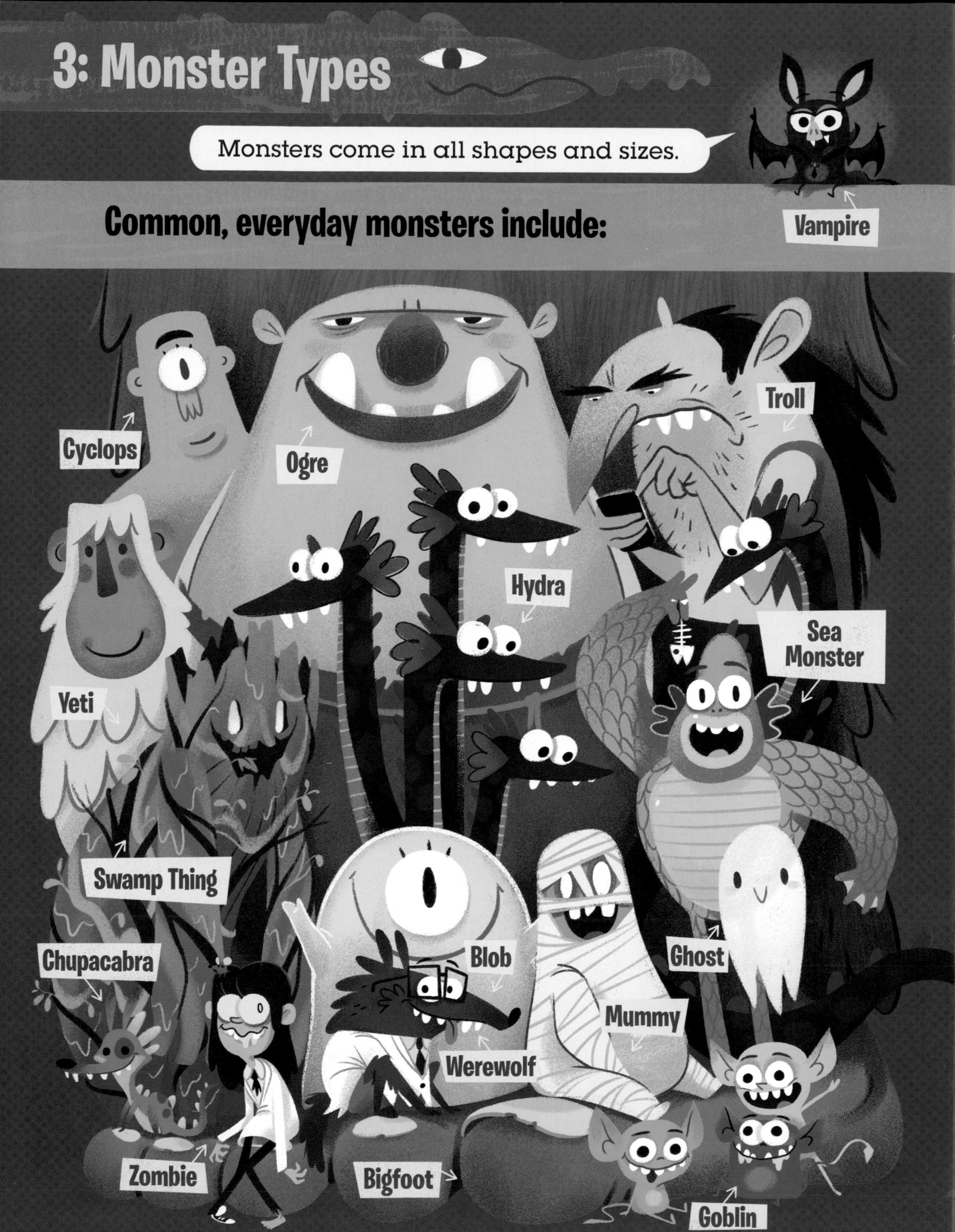

Lesser-known and rare monsters include:

4: Daily Life, Part 1–Weekdays

While monsters love to have a good time, not every day can be a wild rumpus. Monsters have to take care of themselves, and it's not always easy!

With all those teeth, many monsters find themselves back in the dentist's chair again and again.

While some monsters spend their time butt naked, other monsters go through clothing at a fast rate.

Whether it's overgrown fur or out-of-control claws, some monsters need constant grooming to look their most horrifying!

Riding the bus or shopping at the market can be tricky when you're a monster. Good thing there's . . .

Sal's Bargain-Price Human Disguises!

Your one-stop shop for all things human!

MONSTER DEALS!

- Costumes
- Masks
- Odors
- Legs
- Hats

Every monster's #1 choice when needing to be out among humans.

- Rated 4.5 on MonsterAdvisor
- Satisfaction scare-anteed

*Must be a monster to redeem.
Only valid at Haunted Hills location.

4: Daily Life, Part 2–Weekends

Favorite monster activities include:

Competitive game nights

Arm wrestling

Scare-offs

Stand-up comedy

Cooking

Scare-aoke

5: Diet

It's no secret that monsters love to eat! Each monster has its own tastes, and these can differ widely.

A study published in the *Monster Science Journal* shared some dishes that all monsters can agree are drool-worthy.
Pickled ant ice cream
Sewage soup
Grilled sneeze sandwich
Spicy dirty laundry sandwich with extra dog fur
Clam pudding with fish heads
BLT—bugs, lizards, and toenails on a sesame seed bun
Superb!
NOM!
NOM!

6: Habitats and Homes

Common items found in a zombie's home:

* Cooking cauldron
* Spider garden
* Personal slime tub
* Pet alligator
* Cozy coffin bed

7: Monster History

Throughout the ages, monsters have played a role in history, from prehistoric times to the present day.

Down in the Unnatural History Cryptorium, we find the Hall of Famous Monsters.
DR. UNDEROOS: First monster to wear underpants
SMOOCHY THE TERRIBLE: World's cutest monster
HOOVES HAMINGTON: First were-pig
IRIS THE SECOND: First cyclops with two eyes
TOFU CAULIFLOWER: First vegetarian zombie
SPIKE THE FRIENDLY: First monster to be friends with a human
INVISI-BILL: World's smallest monster
BLECHULA: First blood-intolerant vampire
OAT BLOOD

8: Fears

It's hard to imagine a monster having anything to be scared of, but monsters can have all types of fears. Don't even get me started on garlic!

Mummies are terrified of playful puppies.

Sea monsters have a phobia of sand getting between their toes.

Gromps have a deep fear of beards.

Werewolves freak out when they hear a vacuum.

If there is one thing that spooks all monsters more than anything else, it's

HUMANS.

They are unpredictable and sneaky and seem to always have it out for monsters.

It only takes one human to yell "MONSTER!" And before you can say "Dracula's underpants," there's a full-on human freak-out.

Monsters are very wary of getting too close to a human, as they never know how humans will react.

9: Monster-Human Interactions

It's not uncommon to find out you're roommates with a ghost, goblin, or gremlin, down in the basement or stuffed in your closet.

It's a basic fact that one in every three homes has a monster hiding under a bed. What are they doing under there? Take a look for yourself!

Am I going to be eaten?

While monsters may send a chill down your spine, the truth is most of them are completely harmless. In fact, many monsters are working hard to change humans' negative view of them.

Like anyone, though, monsters can have an off day or be in a bad mood, and that may include swallowing a mailman or eating a car.

If you encounter a monster, it's a good idea to follow these three rules:

1. Don't point, stare, or call them a monster. That's just rude.
2. Don't try petting them. Humans are always trying to pet everything!
3. Be cool and don't panic. Monsters can smell fear, and it smells really, really bad.

Keeping those things in mind, it should be easy to become BFFs with any monster you meet!

10: Diploma

You've made it to the end without losing any brains or body parts! You have earned the right to be an honorary Monster Scientist.

Next time you hear a bump in the night, think back to all you have learned here, and remember: It's probably more scared of you than you are of it.

The only thing left to do is howl in celebration!

Monstronomy
Diploma
successfully finished this course
and earned the haunted title of
Monster Scientist
It is your duty to study, protect, and care for
all the monsters of the world.
Mcfang
Professor Batula McFang
HOWLSWORTH
Professor Howlsworth
BLOBBINS
Professor Blobbins
BRaiinnns!
Tina